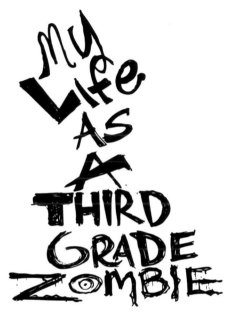

My Life As A Third Grade Zombie

C.M. Longmeyer   Illustrations by Dexter Blanding

GALLOPADE

Book design and illustrations: Dexter Blanding
Ebook manager: John Hanson
Project oversight: Paige Muh

Dedicated to Christina, Grant, Avery, Ella, Evan and Sadie Hope, my little zombies!

Other My Life as a Third Grade...Books

My Life as a Third Grade Werewolf

My Life as a Third Grade Vampire

I'm a zombie.
It's true. I'm not making it up.
I was born in Haiti.
Haiti is a country that was once lovely,
my grandfather says.
Today it's poor and war-torn.
I'm glad we don't live there anymore.

No, I don't look gross like you think.
My arms and legs aren't all akimbo (well, most of the time.)
My stare isn't blank, usually.
And there are no dirt or blood smears on my skin
and clothes, at least no more than any other third grade boy.

I know. It sounds like I'm a boring zombie. But I'm not.
There's a girl in my class who's a zombie too. Maria.
Her skin is grayer than mine and she does have
a blank look on her face, mostly during math.
She walks sort of funny.

In Haiti, my grandmother used to tease me with a voodoo doll.
You know what that is.
She'd stick a pin ("Ouch!")
and tell me I was a bad ("Ouch!") boy, and we would laugh.
It really didn't hurt, well, not too much.
It was much more painful when she grabbed me and kissed me on
my cheeks. *In front of my friends.*

At school they know I'm a zombie.
I'm always getting called to the office.
"Joe," says Mr. Ernie, the principal.
"Dougie Jones in second grade says you bit his neck
and sucked his blood."
Mr. Ernie always looks mortified.

"I did not," I say. "That's what vampires do.
I am not a vampire, I'm a zombie, Mr. Ernie. You know that."

"Oh, yeah," Mr. Ernie always says, looking sorry.
"I forgot. Never mind. Go back to class."

I trudge back down the hall but stop to glare at Dougie Jones sitting in his classroom. He has mud from the playground smeared on his neck.

My teacher, Ms. Bogus, knows I'm a zombie.
She seems a little disappointed in me, like maybe I should
look or act more zombie-ish.
She does not know that Maria is a zombie.
She likes Maria.

The next day at school, the PA system calls me to the office.
I sigh. Mr. Ernie is waiting for me.
"Joe, Ernestine Brown in the fourth grade swears that you
said you were going to put a bolt through her head.
That is not acceptable behavior."

"Mr. Ernie..." I say and he sighs.
"A bolt through the head is Frankenstein. I do not do bolts.
I am a zombie. Ok?"
Mr. Ernie does not look too sure about this, but he just says,
"Ok, Joe, please return to class."

Every time I get called to the office (even if I am not guilty as charged), they have to email my Mom a note.
Then when I get home, grandma's old voodoo doll is waiting for me.

"Mom," I promise. "Ouch!
I did not do those...ouch!...things. Ouch!".
My Mom always believes me. She hugs me and kisses me on my cheeks, leaving her red lipstick all over.
At least my friends are not here to see this.

Soon it is Halloween. There is a school dance. Yuck!
I'm a third grade boy. I do not like girls. I do not like dances.
I do like my costume. I dress as a zombie.
So does Maria. We look pretty cool.
The other kids ask, "Where did you get your cool costume?"
I just shrug my shoulders. They ask Maria the same question.
She just blushes.

At the Halloween dance, the girls dance together.
The boys stand around.
Finally, Ms. Bogus makes each boy ask a girl to dance.
I ask Maria.
She shrugs her shoulders but takes my hand.
When we start to dance, something happens.
My arms and legs are akimbo. So are Maria's.
We dance herky-jerky to the music.
Everyone stops to watch. They think we look cool.
We win the dance contest
and the best costume boy and girl contest.

The next day, as usual, I get called to the office.
"What now?" I ask Mr. Ernie.

"Bobby Evans says that at the dance last night you clawed
his back with your hairy hands," Mr. Ernie complains.
I showed Mr. Ernie my hands. "Not me.
That is a werewolf. I'm a zombie, remember?"
Mr. Ernie nods sadly and sends me back to class.

On the way to class I stop by the boy's bathroom.
I look in the mirror.
I am surprised to see that my face is a little gray.
My lips are a little darker.
And my elbows are stuck out a little, sort
of the way Maria's are. *Hmm*, I think. *Hmm*.

SLAM!!

After school my Mom gets all over me.
"Why did you not wash your face?"
"I did, Mom, I...Ouch!...promise."
She grabs a dishrag and begins to wipe my face.
"Ouch! Ouch!"
I run to my room and close the door.
It is hard to be a third grade zombie.

Tonight in the newspaper, I see an ad.
It is for kid actors for a television show called
The Zombie Kidz™.
The next day I do not go to school. I go to the audition.

When I walk up to the casting desk, they look at me funny.
I shrug my shoulders.
"I have my own make-up and costume," I say.

"Me, too," says a voice behind me. I turn around. It is Maria.
We both audition and get parts as kid zombies.
They call zombies the *Walking Dead*, you know.
It is fun to be around so many zombies.

I go home and take a bath.
The next morning I look in the mirror. I look like a zombie.
I act like a zombie. I walk like a zombie.
I try to sneak out of the house so my Mom will not see me,
but she does. I shrug my shoulders, hoping to avoid being
her voodoo doll pincushion. Mom just pats my shoulder.
"Have a good day at school, son," she says.

At school, I sneak into the classroom and sit at my desk.
Ms. Bogus ignores me.
There is no call from the principal's office.
Suddenly, someone taps me on the shoulder.
I turn around. It is Maria.
She looks like a zombie, too.

"What's happened to us?" I ask her.
Maria smiles. "I guess we just finally grew up into being real
walking dead zombies."
"Cool," I say. "Cool."

Maria hooks her akimbo arm in mine, and we walk to
the cafeteria for lunch. We pass Mr. Ernie.
"Hi, Mr. Ernie," I say. Mr. Ernie just smiles at me.
"Hi, Joe," he says, and walks on down the hall.
And that, was that.

I was free to be me. Finally. And so was Maria.

About the Author

Carole Marsh Longmeyer has been writing fiction, non-fiction, and curriculum for kids for more than 30 years. Her favorite things are humor, great art (see Dexter Blanding, below!), introducing kids to little-known facts and new words. She hopes this story of self-acceptance is helpful in this way too-judgmental world. You can reach her at carole@gallopade.com.

About the Artist

Dexter Blanding is a graduate of Savannah College of Art and Design where he majored in Sequential Art and minored in Story Boarding. His passions include comedy, great storytelling (see Carole Marsh Longmeyer, above!) comics and making people smile. He hopes that his art brightens up somebody's day!

A Glossary of Zombie Words

akimbo: to have your arms and legs bent at odd angles; do it!

audition: to try out for a part in a play, movie or other performance

casting: picking an actor or actress for a role

Haiti: a lovely Caribbean nation that has an interesting history and is prone to earthquakes

PA: Public Announcement

shrug: to pull your shoulders up towards your ears; do it!

trudge: to walk slowly with heavy steps; try it!

Voodoo dolls are little cloth or string dolls. My grandmother used one for a pincushion.
She used to tease me that she was going to stick me and I would become a zombie.

Zombie Tee Art Activity

Create a zombie tee shirt, just for fun. Sketch it on a separate piece of paper.

Zombie Writing Activity

Write a poem, story, rap song, or something else about a zombie.

Questions for Discussion and Debate

1. What do you think this story is really about?

2. At what age do we begin to feel different, or like we have to conform, or like we don't want to stand out for our individuality or unique nature?

3. At what age do we think it's cool to be ourselves and not worry so much about what other people think?

4. When someone in class is "different," are you nice to them, or avoid them? Why?

5. If you are the "different" person, how do you want to be treated?

6. How did Joe and Maria finally find acceptance as third grade zombies?